Mahogany Tales
Modern Urban Retellings of Classic Tales

By Chanel Hardy

I0621493

Ciara: A Cinderella Retelling

"Hurry up and finish cutting that grass girl!" Wanda yelled from inside the house. She stood in the doorway, with one hand on her hip, and the other fanning herself trying to get some relief from the smoldering heat. She slammed the screen door as she went back inside, frustrated that Ciara was taking too long to mow the lawn.

Ciara took her sweet time cutting the grass, even if it meant suffering in 90-degree temps with awful humidity adding to her misery. Anything was better than being in that house with her stepmother and annoying stepsisters. Two years ago, Ciara moved from Chicago to Georgia when her father passed away. Having no other living relatives, his ex-wife Wanda was the only one who could take Ciara in. It was either Wanda or foster care. Ciara hated Wanda and her two twin daughters Jasmine and Jamilla. From the minute Ciara set foot in their home, they treated her like a slave. Making her do all the housework, cleaning up after all three of them, day and night. They also made her sleep in the attic, which was dark and dusty. All Ciara had to do, was last another few weeks until her eighteenth birthday, which was also her graduation day, when she could finally be on her own. What Wanda and her daughters didn't know, was that Ciara's father had left money in a secret account for Ciara, in her name to receive when she became a legal adult.

Ciara wiped the sweat from her forehead, as she turned off the lawnmower and dragged it over to the shed to put away. She walked back inside the house, where Jasmine and Jamilla sat lazily on the sofa watching TV.

"About time! The laundry needs to be done. We have nothing to wear to school tomorrow." Jasmine screeched at Ciara.

"I've never seen someone take so long to do simple chores." Jamilla chimed in, swinging her foot back and forth on the arm of the sofa.

Ciara rolled her eyes. "How would you know? You don't do anything but sit in front of the TV all day long."

Wanda walked into the living room from the kitchen, overhearing Ciara's remark. "What did I tell you about talking to my girls like that? You've been in this house for two years now, and you still haven't learned any respect."

"Respect? They don't respect anybody!" Ciara shouted.

"Who do you think you're talking to?" Jasmine jumped in to defend her mother.

"Shut up! I wasn't talking to you!" Ciara shot back.

"Watch your mouth! Don't you have chores to do? I think you need to go do them before I smack you!" A vein emerged from Wanda's forehead.

Jasmine and Jamilla laughed as Ciara stormed off, running up to the attic where she could be alone. Once she got up there, she threw herself on her bed and started crying, her face shoved into her pillows. So many times, she thought about running away, but being a minor on her own with nowhere to go, wasn't a smart idea. A few weeks felt like a million years living under the roof of a vile woman like Wanda. She made Ciara's life a living nightmare, all out of spite because she and Ciara's father divorced on bad terms. But it would all be over soon, and Ciara would finally be free.

* * *

Ciara was startled out of her sleep as Wanda used a broom to bang against the ceiling to wake her up for school. She rolled over, turning off her alarm clock before it buzzed.

"I'M UP!" She yelled back so Wanda could stop banging like a crazy woman. She pulled the covers off of her and made her way to the downstairs bathroom to shower. She was exhausted, having spent the entire night doing the family's laundry, washing dishes, and cleaning the kitchen after dinner. After her shower, as she was getting dressed Wanda yelled again for her to hurry outside before the school bus arrived. Ciara had almost forgotten to grab her gold charm bracelet. It was given to her by her father as a Christmas gift when she was fourteen. It was one of the only things she had left that reminded her of him, and of the great life she had before his death. She quickly grabbed it from her nightstand and clamped it onto her wrist before grabbing her backpack and heading downstairs.

As soon as the bus arrived, Jasmine and Jamilla got on first, shoving Ciara out of their way. Jasmine and Jamilla took their usual seats in the front with their friends, and Ciara walked toward the back, sitting by herself as usual. She was a quiet girl, who never took the time to make any friends and often kept to herself. Being a city girl, Ciara didn't blend in with the southern folks and their ho-hum culture.

The bell rang for the first period as Ciara grabbed her books for Science class. The morning announcements started as the principal gave his usual speech.

"...also, seniors don't forget ladies and gentlemen to put in your picks for prom king and queen by this afternoon! I hope you're all looking forward to prom this Saturday night!"

Ciara wasn't looking forward to it. She wanted to go, but Wanda wouldn't allow it. Even if she could, she had no date, so it was a pointless fancy anyway. Just as she closed her locker, she noticed from the corner of her eye, Brandon Charles walking toward her. He was one of the popular boys. Rich, attractive, and well-mannered. But unlike the other boys, he stood out. Brandon Charles was different, he was polite, and treated everyone he encountered with the utmost respect. There wasn't a student or school staff member that didn't love him. This is why Ciara could never understand how a guy like him was still single. She stood there, awkward, with her book in hand as he walked up to her.

"Hey, Ciara!" Brandon approached her, and she became distracted by his pearly white smile and his dimples, almost forgetting to say hello back. His brown skin always looked so smooth and creamy, like peanut butter.

"Oh, Hi." She replied, snapping back to reality.

"You look nice today. That hairstyle really fits you." He said, pointing to her bantu knots.

"Oh, thank you, Brandon." She didn't think too much of his compliment, as it was a part of his personality to be charming. But it still made her feel warm and fuzzy inside, as she grinned.

"Since you're on your way to science, as well as I, I just wanted to ask if you took any notes from yesterday? I think we're gonna have a pop quiz today."

"Yes, I did." Ciara opened her science notebook and flipped to the page containing notes from the day before, and handed it to him. "Here you go."

"Thanks. Well, let's go. We should be getting to class don't you think?"

Ciara cleared her throat. "Umm, we?"

"Yes. We have the same first-period science class, remember?" He shook his head, amused by her awkwardness.

"Oh yeah."

He walked ahead as Ciara trailed behind. Admiring him as he led them to class.

As they walked in, the class was preparing to dissect baby pigs. Brandon took a seat near the back, and Ciara sat in her usual seat in the front row.

"Alright now, there is no time to waste. Pick a partner and prepare your stations." The teacher demanded. Everyone started partnering with their friends, most of the girls eyeing Brandon to see who he would pick as his partner. He chose the girl that was already sitting next to him, Amanda. Ciara just sat there, waiting for the last student to be paired with her by default. Nearly the entire class was paired up, except Ciara. One of the students was out sick, so that left Ciara as the odd one out.

"Ciara looks like you don't have a partner." The teacher gazed around at everyone to find a pair to stick Ciara with. "Why don't you go work with Brandon and Amanda?"

Ciara's heart started pounding as she turned around, looking back at Brandon, who was waving in her direction, and Amanda, who didn't look too pleased to have to share. She got up and walked to the last row, sitting on Brandon's left. Amanda looked at her, swinging her long braids and rolling her eyes.

"Hey, friend! Looks like there's three of us today." Brandon said enthusiastically.

"ha-ha, yeah, looks to be so." Ciara scratched her head and fiddled with a loose curl that hung freely in the back of her head, trying not to make eye contact. Every time she did, nervousness snuck its way up her spine and her palms got sweaty.

The entire time they worked on the baby pig, Ciara couldn't help but stare at the smooth skin on his arms. She was too distracted by his good looks to focus on the assignment.

After class had dismissed, she grabbed her books and hurried to her locker. Brandon ran after her, catching up to her as she opened it.

"Hey, you left so fast, I forgot to give you your notebook back." He held out his hand, handing it back to her.

"Thanks."

"You're welcome."

Jasmine strutted by, on her way to her next period class, taking a quick pause to talk to Brandon. "Hey Brandon, still no date for the prom this weekend?" She twirled her hair, smacking on her bubblegum. "Ugh." She looked at Ciara in disgust, who just turned to face her locker in embarrassment.

"No, not yet." He replied.

"Well, I'm still available." She caressed his arm, giving him a wink before prancing off to catch up with her friends.

"That's your sister, right?" He asked Ciara.

"Stepsister, yes. I hate her."

"Wow, I can't possibly imagine why. She's so… nice." They both laughed at his sarcasm. The bell rang, and their moment ceased.

"I'll see ya." He walked off, heading to his next class.

"Bye," Ciara said softly under her breath, as she watched him leave. Brandon was every girl's dream, but for a girl like Ciara, a dream was all she had.

* * *

"Ya'll look so good! I love it!" Wanda cheered with excitement as she watched Jasmine and Jamilla twirl, and pose in their elegant gowns while she took pictures. "Those other girls better watch out!" She laughed, snapping her finger and hugging her daughters.

It was Saturday night, Prom Night. Ciara watched from the kitchen as she swept the floor. Looking at the girls' model in front of their mother in their bright blue and orange dresses. Ciara thought the dresses were hideous, but she knew better than to say anything out loud.

"Brandon won't be able to resist all this tonight!" Jasmine said with confidence, with her hands on her hips. Ciara snorted, trying to hold in her laughter from overhearing Jasmine's comment. All three of them paused and turned around looking at Ciara.

"What's so funny?" Wanda asked, raising an eyebrow.

Ciara instantly regretted her outburst, wishing she could take it back. The last thing she wanted to deal with, was a fight with them.

"Nothing." She replied, still sweeping.

"It didn't sound like nothing!" Wanda snapped.

Jasmine walked closer toward the kitchen. "She's just jealous because Brandon wants me." Her eyes glared at Ciara.

"Jealous? I'd never be jealous of you! You're delusional, Brandon would never like a girl like you."

Jasmine's eyes widened. "Oh, let me guess, he goes for girls like you? Ugly, nappy-headed skinny girls with flat butts." Jasmine, Jamilla, and Wanda broke out in laughter. Ciara clenched the broom handle, furious, but there was nothing she could do. This moment just added itself to her long list of reasons why she loathed them all and hated every second of living in that house.

"Hurry up in that kitchen, you've got other stuff to do," Wanda told Ciara.

Jasmine and Jamilla grabbed their purses and headed toward the door, as their limo waited outside. Once the girls were out the door, Wanda walked into the kitchen, slowly approaching Ciara as she put the broom and dustpan away in the corner. Ciara turned around, her and Wanda standing eye to eye.

"What now? I'm done with the kitchen." Ciara backed away slowly.

"You're just like your father. A loser, a nobody." Wanda looked her up and down, before turning around and leaving the kitchen. Ciara didn't even have it in her to be angry at this point. All she felt was pain. She ran up to the attic, not even caring about the rest of the housework. She plopped down on the floor next to her bed, with her face buried into her hands, crying.

"Dad, I wish you were here."

She then felt cold, scrawny hands clench her arms. She screamed, jumping in fear, and leaping backward onto her bed, falling to the floor on the opposite side. She sprang up, looking to see who else was there. "WHO WAS THAT?" she looked around frantically, not seeing anyone.

"Calm down child, I'm right here." A female voice said from behind her. The woman placed her hand on Ciara's shoulder. Ciara turned around, screaming.

"WHO ARE YOU?"

"I'm your spirit mother. You can call me, Adah."

The woman was short, dark, and very thin. She had long, white wild, thick hair that bounced as she moved. Her skin was wrinkly, and her eyes were light brown, like honey. She was dressed in all white, her dress torn at the hem, and sleeveless. She was barefoot, which made Ciara think she was a crazy homeless woman who had snuck into her house somehow.

"How did you get in here?!" Ciara began to back away.

"Don't worry about that, it's not important. What's important, is you."

Ciara was confused. "What? What are you talking about?"

"I was sent here by the Gods to grant your request." Adah walked slowly toward Ciara, with a tranquil smile, and her hand extended, showing that she meant no harm.

"My request? About my father?"

Adah laughed. "Silly girl, I am a spirit mother, Not a God. Even Gods themselves could not bring a man back from the dead."

Ciara couldn't wrap her head around what was going on. "Look lady, I don't know how you got in here, but you need to leave. Now."

Adah was standing a few inches away from Ciara. She placed her cold, skinny hands on Ciara's face, moving her head from left to right, examining her closely. "Pretty girl, strong face, like a warrior!" She smiled, looking Ciara dead in the eyes. "But I can tell, that there is hate in your heart. Fire in your soul, we must put out that fire."

"Huh? What are you talking about-"

Before Ciara could finish, she looked down and was covered in Turquoise from head to toe. Her jaw dropped, as she jumped out of the grasp of Adah, and stumbled backward from the sequin-covered heels that were on her feet. She sat on the floor, grabbing the sides of her dress. It was a long silk gown, smooth like the clear blue waters of the ocean that surrounded a tropical island. It had long sleeves, with a wide V-neck shape revealing her shoulders. She touched her ears, where diamond chandelier earrings hung from her lobes. Her hair was pulled back in an elegant braided bun.

"Magnificent!" Adah yelled, with her arms in the air.

Ciara got up from the floor. "How did you... I look... But I don't understand." Ciara was in awe.

"You don't have to understand." Adah smiled. "Oh, don't forget about this!" She snapped her finger, and Ciara's charm bracelet appeared on her left wrist.

"What about Wanda? She'll kill me if I leave!"

"Don't worry about her. I've got her under a sleeping spell. It'll hold until midnight. Not even Armageddon could wake that woman."

Ciara then remembered about Jasmine and Jamilla. There was no way she could show up at prom without them noticing.

"Oh, and don't worry about those stepsisters of yours either. They won't be making it there. Unfortunately for them, their driver caught a flat!" Adah laughed, grinning from ear to ear. Ciara laughed along with her, covering her mouth trying not to be too loud. The thought of Jasmine and Jamilla missing the prom was hilarious.

"Oh, and I must tell you, there is only one condition."

Ciara stopped giggling, as Adah's facial expression turned serious.

"No one at Prom will have any memory of this after tonight. Except you of course. They will remember prom, but a different version of it. One where you weren't there."

"Wait, why?"

"That's just how it must be, my child."

"But I don't understand, how is that possible?"

Adah walked toward her, wrapping her arms around her and hugging her tightly. "Anything is possible with the power of love. Now go, he's waiting for you."

Ciara hugged her back. "How can I ever repay you?" She asked softly. Within the blink of an eye, Adah was gone, and so was the attic.

* * *

Ciara looked around and realized that she was at the Chestnut Grand Hotel, where the prom was being held. She looked around to see if anyone had noticed her sudden entrance, but the coast was clear. She looked at her reflection through one of the glass doors and couldn't believe how beautiful she really looked. She had never been this dressed up before.

Straight down the hall, was the entrance to the ballroom. Nervous, she walked toward the double doors not knowing what to expect, or how her classmates would react once they saw her inside. She approached the doors, took a deep breath, and as she reached out to open them, someone called her name from behind.

"Ciara?"

She turned around, and it was Brandon. Her eyes lit up, and she froze in place.

He walked closer toward her. "Ciara, you… you look beautiful."

He stood in front of her, gazing at her up and down. His bright white teeth shined through as he smiled at her, wearing an all-white tux.

"Brandon! Hello… Umm… it's nice to s- see you." Ciara said, stumbling over her words.

"I'm surprised to see you here. Are you alone?" He asked.

"Who me? Oh, yes. I came alone." She replied, with her head down.

"Oh, cool. I didn't bring a date either." He buttoned the top of his shirt, adjusting his vest. Ciara looked up at him, and his eyes were still set on her. "Well, here I am, and here you are. No pressure, but would you like to be my date, Ciara?" He extended his arm out to her.

Without saying another word, she took his arm, he opened the double doors, and in they walked, together.

The doors behind them didn't even close before every set of eyes in the room were on them. Ciara became numb. Nervous, she was never used to this much attention. Brandon placed his right hand gently on her lower back. "It's okay." He whispered to her softly. "Let's dance."

She looked up at him, he looked back. Smiling at her with his pearly whites shining so bright. Suddenly, the nervous feeling went away, and as he led her to the middle of the dance floor, everyone disappeared. In Ciara's mind, she and Brandon were the only ones in the room. Students cleared their path, and Ciara stood facing Brandon. He grabbed her left hand, with his other hand holding her side. A new song had just started playing over the speakers, and they moved together in sync with the music.

Coming out of her light trance, she became aware again that they were in a room full of their peers, and everyone was staring. Mostly, other girls who didn't look too pleased to see them together. Their eyes filled with jealousy as they watched the most popular and most wanted boy in school dancing with the least popular and most undesirable girl in school. Ciara looked down, not to make eye contact with any of them and getting too nervous again to look at Brandon.

"Don't worry about them." Brandon could tell their nasty looks were intimidating her.

"I'm trying." She looked up at him.

"You really do look amazing tonight, Ciara."

She smiled, giggling a little. She still couldn't believe any of this was happening. "Thank you."

The slow song they were dancing to was ending, and an upbeat hip-hop song started playing. This got the other students hyped, and they all started dancing, no longer interested in Brandon or Ciara.

"This is my song!" Brandon started dancing, hyping Ciara up to dance along. She was shy, and not much of a dancer, but went along with the beat.

"Are you thirsty?" He asked.

"Sure."

He grabbed her hand, and they walked over to the refreshments to grab punch. As he grabbed two cups and filled them up, Ciara looked to her right and noticed Amanda standing there with two of her friends. They whispered to each other, before rolling their eyes at Ciara and heading in the other direction. Ciara tried her best to brush it off but wasn't good at pretending things didn't bother her. Brandon handed her one of the cups and noticed that she looked bothered.

"Why don't we get out of here and go somewhere quiet." He said, sipping from his cup.

"I'd like that." She replied, relieved to be getting a chance to be alone with him, and away from the crowd.

With their cups still in hand, they walked out of the ballroom, and down the hall heading out to the courtyard. It was dark but lit with fluorescent lights hanging from the bushes. They walked over to a nearby bench that was next to a fountain and sat down.

"I should've asked, but I was afraid." Said Brandon, looking up at the sky.

"Huh?" Ciara was confused by what he meant.

"Prom. I should've asked you to prom weeks ago. But, I was nervous. I didn't think you'd say yes."

Ciara couldn't believe what she was hearing. "Me? You... wanted to ask... me?" She nearly choked on her punch."

"Yes." He turned toward her, looking into her big brown eyes. "I've always liked you. When I asked for your notes the other day, I didn't need them. I just wanted an excuse to talk to you. I intentionally avoided having a date tonight, in hopes that I would see you here."

Ciara stood up, she started to get knots in her stomach. She wasn't sure if this was real or some big joke. "Look, I don't know if this is some joke the other girls put you up too, but-"

"No. Why would you think that?" He stood up, next to her.

"Well… because, guys like you don't like girls like me." She was fiddling with her fingers, avoiding eye contact.

"Guys like me?"

"Yeah."

He took her hand. "I'm popular, girls like me, I can't control those things, and I didn't ask for them. But those things don't determine how I feel about you."

They were facing each other. Ciara felt butterflies and a warm feeling rushed through her as she squeezed his hand firmly. "I like you too, a lot actually."

He smiled at her, and she covered her face with the palms of her hands. Before she could say another word, he removed her hands away from her face and kissed her. It was a moment she had only ever dreamed of. His lips were soft, and his hands were too as he gently held the sides of her face in a moment that was both enchanting and unforgettable.

An hour passed, as they walked around the courtyard, holding hands, engaging in conversation, and getting to know each other outside of being classmates who had shared no more than a few words at school. As it turned out, they had quite a bit of things in common.

"After graduation, I'm moving to LA, to work with my dad. I'm taking over his company after he retires in three years" Brandon told her.

"That sounds amazing."

"What about you?"

Ciara wasn't sure how to respond. "I don't know. I won't be here, that's for sure. I can't wait to get away from my stepmom and stepsisters."

"I'm sorry you have to put up with them." He tried to empathize with her unfortunate home life.

"It's cool. I'm almost eighteen. My birthday is the same day as graduation. Then I'll be on my own, and never looking back." She stood by the fountain, looking into the water.

"Well, wherever you decide to go, I hope we can keep in touch. I don't want graduation to be the end of us." He stood by the fountain, next to her, touching her shoulder.

She looked up at him. "Me either."

"Maybe you can come to LA too!" He suggested with excitement.

Ciara was surprised by his suggestion. "LA? With you? I'd love that!" She then remembered what Adah told her. After tonight, no one would remember any of this. Not even Brandon. Which means he wouldn't remember about revealing his feelings, or the kiss, or asking her about LA." Her excitement turned to sadness. "But, I can't."

"Why not?"

"It's complicated." Ciara didn't know how to explain.

"But it doesn't have to be." He brushed her chin with his fingers and kissed her again.

As much as she loved this moment, she hated it just as much, knowing that after tonight it would mean nothing. She just enjoyed his embrace and let the emotions from the kiss engulf them both.

"I wanna dance," Ciara said to him. If this night would be their last, she wanted to enjoy it to the fullest. She wanted everyone to witness their newfound love, and make the best of what was left of her amazing night.

"Alright, let's go back inside." Brandon took her hand, and they left the courtyard, and went back to the ballroom, to dance the night away.

The prom ended at eleven on the dot. Brandon offered to drive Ciara home, which was great considering she had no idea how she was getting back home. As they arrived at her house, Brandon stopped the car, and they sat for a few minutes. Ciara still had a good half an hour before Adah's sleeping spell on Wanda had worn off.

"Promise me you'll think about it, going to LA with me."

Ciara didn't have it in her to tell the truth, but it didn't matter. He wouldn't remember any of this anyway. "I promise." She said, leaning over to kiss him one last time.

"See you in school on Monday." He winked at her, smiling.

"See ya Monday." She smiled back, hiding the pain. She got out of the car and hurried toward the door. Looking back one last time as he drove away.

As she walked in, Wanda was still out cold on the couch. There was no sign of the twins, who never made it to prom just like Adah said, but Ciara wasn't worried. She quickly went up to the attic, tossing off her heels and jumping in the bed. She was so exhausted from dancing all night, she drifted off to sleep.

* * *

The next morning, Ciara awoke to her alarm clock buzzing through her ears. Her dress was gone, and she was in her pajamas. Her perfect braided bun was now a matted mess of her bushy hair. All she could think about was Brandon, and the amazing night they shared. Then she realized that he would have no recollection of it when she saw him at school. Her eyes started to tear up.

"CIARA! GET UP!" Wanda yelled from downstairs.

"She frowned, wiping her eyes and getting out of bed. She turned to grab her charm bracelet from her nightstand, only to find it wasn't there.

"Oh, no."

She thought back to last night and realized the last time she saw it was in Brandon's car. It must have slipped off her wrist somehow. She had no idea how she would get it back or explain to him how it ended up in his car.

"CIARA!" Wanda yelled again.

Ciara rushed downstairs to start her chores. Jasmine and Jamilla were still livid about missing prom. Threatening to get the driver fired and to sue the limo company for ruining their night. Ciara, wore a sinister look across her face as she listened to them complain about their horrible night, laughing on the inside.

"Thank you, Adah." She whispered to herself, as she swept the kitchen floor.

* * *

Monday morning, Ciara stood at her locker, grabbing her books for class, hoping she wouldn't run into Brandon, but secretly hoping she would. That's when she noticed him walking in her direction. She didn't know what to do, or how to react. As he got closer, she got nervous and blurted out the only thing she could think of.

"HEY BRANDON!" She said loudly, with a screeching voice. She immediately regretted it.

He paused, caught off guard by her random greeting.

"Hey, Ciara." He waved. One of his friends called for his attention, and he kept on his way down the hall. Ciara slammed her head against her locker, feeling like an idiot. She just wanted the school year to be over already, so she wouldn't have to deal with the pain of loving someone who didn't even remember loving her back.

* * *

Two weeks had passed, and it was graduation day and Ciara's eighteenth birthday. She watched from a distance as Brandon took photos with all his friends and family after the ceremony, looking so happy and proud. Ciara took photos of Jasmine, Jamilla, and Wanda posing together, getting distracted while stealing glances of Brandon. She hadn't spoken to him since that morning by her locker after prom and decided not to approach him about her bracelet, in hopes that he would find it, and inquire about who it belonged to. Still, she had no idea how to explain it being in his car, or if he would even ask.

Finally, Wanda and the girls were done snapping pictures, and it was time to go. She turned around to get one last look at Brandon, wanting so desperately to run over to him and tell him everything, but it was pointless. He'd just think she was crazy, and that's the last thing she wanted. She tried so hard to hold back her tears. In the morning, she would be gone anyway. She was going to the bank to withdraw the money her father left her, packing up and going to the train station heading north. After today, everything and everyone would be behind her. School, this town, Wanda, Jasmine, Jamilla, and even Brandon.

When they got home, Ciara didn't waste any time packing. She grabbed her suitcase from under her bed and started throwing in all her clothes and whatever else could fit. The sooner she packed the better. As she was packing, she noticed Wanda had made her way up to the attic. Standing there with her arms crossed.

"Where do you think you're going, little girl?" She confronted Ciara with a sassy tone.

Ciara was done biting her tongue and didn't care what Wanda had to say. "I'm leaving tomorrow."

"Leaving? Ha! Going where? You have nothing and no one!"

"That's what you think! My father left me money, for when I turned eighteen. Well, now I am. I'm finally out of here."

Wanda eased in closer toward her. "Oh, about that... I withdrew that money months ago." She said with an evil smirk.

"WHAT!" Ciara was furious.

"I found out about that little account your father had for you. You really thought you could keep it a secret, huh?" Wanda laughed. "As your guardian, I had the legal right to withdraw the money. So, it's mine now."

Ciara struck Wanda across the face. Wanda held her cheek in disbelief. "Get out of my house! Now!"

Ciara grabbed her suitcase and left the attic. She bolted past Jasmine, nearly knocking her over and running toward the front door, and heading outside. She dropped her suitcase on the porch and collapsed down next to it. Crying into her lap, not knowing where she would go, or what she would do. Her evil stepmother had taken the one thing she had to start a new life. Now she had nothing.

Suddenly, she heard a car pull up to the house. She lifted her head from her hands to see who it was. She couldn't believe it and thought she was dreaming. It was Brandon. He got out of the car, walking up toward Ciara. She stood on her feet. "Brandon?" She said with a raspy voice, wiping her tears.

"Hey, Ciara. I think I have something that belongs to you?" He held out his hand, and her bracelet hung from his palm.

Her eyes lit up. "My bracelet!"

"I found it while I was cleaning out my car."

She reached out and grabbed it. "But... how did you know it was mine?"

"Prom night. I know it sounds crazy, but when I picked up your bracelet in my car, it was like everything came back to me. I remembered everything. The courtyard, your beautiful blue dress, the kiss. Everything. I can't explain it, but I remember. I remember us."

"There's nothing to explain." She threw her arms around him, pressing her lips against his. It felt like prom night all over again.

He broke their embrace and noticed her suitcase. "Going somewhere?" He asked.

"You tell me."

Brandon grabbed her suitcase. "Our flight leaves next week."

Wanda came storming out, swinging the front door wide open. "What is going on here?!" She looked at Ciara and Brandon, puzzled by what was going on. Jasmine and Jamilla ran to the door, behind her.

"Brandon Charles?!" Jasmine exclaimed, her jaw dropped at the sight of him.

"Goodbye, Wanda. Enjoy the money. I won't be needing it." Ciara grabbed Brandon's hand and they ran to his car, jumping inside as he started the engine and pulled off. Ciara looked back at Wanda and the girls, who were still standing there, watching them disappear in the distance.

"Oh, I almost forgot, Happy Birthday babe," Brandon said to her.

Ciara smiled, as the breeze from the window brushed her face.

"Happy birthday to me too.

Porsha: A Pocahontas Retelling

Porsha sat at a table in the corner of the coffee shop, sipping her chai latte. She was reading "The Help" by Kathryn Stockett. The noise from the busy espresso machines & baristas yelling out orders was no distraction for her whenever she was deep into a good book. She was so into it, her eyes glued to page 186, that she didn't even notice a young man trying to get her attention.

"Excuse me?" Said the young man, rather loudly this time.

Porsha lifted her head, a little bothered by his interruption. "Yeah?"

"Sorry, I was just wondering if you were using this chair?" He asked, with his hand on the top of the black wooden chair.

"Uhm, no." She replied, immediately going back to her reading.

"Thanks!" He started to drag the chair back to another table, then paused, when he noticed the book she was reading. "Good movie."

Porsha lifted her head again. "What?"

"The movie, The Help. I loved it. Haven't read the book yet though." The young man said.

Porsha was wondering why this guy she didn't know, a tall, medium built, blue-eyed blonde boy was still talking to her and wouldn't go away. "Oh, that's nice."

The young man could tell that Porsha was too into her book to care about what he was saying, so he dragged the chair back to his table, leaving her alone. Suddenly her phone rang, it was her friend Brittany. Porsha closed her book, with her bookmark in place and answered the call.

"Hey what's up." She answered.

"Girl! You won't believe what I'm looking at!" Brittany exclaimed.

"What?"

"The Riley Gibbs Recreation Center! There is a sign in front of it that says condos are coming soon! They're tearing it down!"

"Yo! You playing?!"

Porsha was furious. But underneath her anger, she wasn't surprised. DC had been slowly going through gentrification the past few years. It started with white twenty-year old's moving into the city for college, pursuing government jobs after graduation. Then a black-owned business closing here and there. Within two years, there was a Starbucks at the corner of Porsha's block. A fancy coffee shop in a predominately black urban area always sealed the deal.

"We grew up at that rec center! Where are the neighborhood kids supposed to go now? That raggedy playground up the street where they can get shot? Oh, no wait. That'll be a Starbucks next week too, so they won't have to worry." Brittany said sarcastically.

"Brit, I'm at the coffee shop on 10th street. Let me finish my coffee and I'll talk to you a little later."

"Alright, cool."

Porsha hung up the phone and suddenly lost the urge to finish her book. Although gentrification wasn't anything new, the thought of a place that meant a lot to her, and to most kids who grew up in the neighborhood being torn down, still hurt. She put her book inside her bag, tossed the last bit of her drink in a nearby garbage can, and left.

***

Porsha sat at the breakfast table, her father Brian, a DCPD officer read the local newspaper while he drank his coffee. "This place is changing more and more every day. Don't even feel like home anymore." He said as he read an article about the Riley Gibbs rec center closing. The local government was selling the building, and it was scheduled to be demolished in three weeks. He flipped to the next page, where another article talked about how the city had "thrived" and improved so much in the last decade. Brian grunted at what he saw.

"I can't believe the rec center is closing. This sucks." Porsha told her father.

"You know these white folks can't wait to take away everything we have and erase our city's culture." Her father said, still reading the paper.

"I mean, I understand wanting to make the city better, uplifting the local economy, but I'm starting to feel I'm being pushed out of my home. Most of us are. When they're done redeveloping, where are the low-class members of the community supposed to go?" Porsha pushed around the eggs on her plate with her fork. "I don't wanna sell our house. Or move."

"Nobody is selling anything or going anywhere." Her father said sternly. He sat his paper down and took a sip of his coffee. "Not yet anyway."

"Dad!"

"What? Don't tell me you wouldn't want to move somewhere quiet, or warm. Florida maybe?"

Porsha grunted at his suggestions. "Florida is humid and sticky. Gross."

"Well whether we like it or not, the city is changing. We either adapt eventually or move on." Her father got up from his seat and placed his half-empty cup in the sink." I'm gonna go to the gym. What are you going to be up to today?" He asked.

"I was going to go by the coffee shop and read for a while. Then hang out with Brittney."

"Alright then. See you later."

"Bye, dad."

Her father left the kitchen, his newspaper was still on the table. She could see the article about the rec center from where she was sitting. All around her she had to watch as her home changed more and more every day. She couldn't do anything about businesses that decided to sell or were priced out of their property, but the rec center was different. It was funded by the city, so there was still a chance that it could be saved. Porsha suddenly had an idea & couldn't wait to tell Brittney.

***

"Good morning! How may I help you!" Greeted the barista at the cash register.

Porsha walked up, not even glancing at the menu. She ordered the same drink every day. "One medium Chai latte with soy please." She dug in her purse to get her wallet, feeling around her junk only to find that it was missing. "Umm… hold on please." She said to the barista. She searched her purse again, pulling out pens and lotion bottles but no sign of her wallet. Then she remembered that she left it at home on her dresser when she was switching bags. "Oh crap, I left my wallet."

The barista looked at her awkwardly. Embarrassed, Porsha began to leave the line, until someone came up to the register, and placed a credit card on the counter.

"I got it. Add a venti iced coffee to that as well. No sweetener please."

Porsha looked over, and it was the young man from yesterday. The one who asked for the chair. He was standing there, smiling at her. "Thanks for that, but you didn't have to." She said to him.

"It's no issue." He replied, still smiling at her, as the cashier rang up the order and handed him his card back. Not sure how to feel about his nice gesture, Porsha walked over to the bar to wait for her drink. After putting his card away, he followed.

"I'm John, by the way, I remember you from yesterday." Introducing himself to her.

"Hi." Porsha gave him a cheesy slight smile with a quick glance, not wanting to make eye contact.

"I never got your name."

"I didn't give it." She said with a snarky tone.

John picked up on her attitude and decided to stop talking. The store was busy, so their drinks were taking longer than usual. Porsha realized that she had maybe been a little harsh toward him when he was only trying to be nice. After all, she did need that chai latte.

"Porsha."

"I'm sorry?"

"My name is Porsha."

"Oh, well, hello Porsha." John smiled.

"Hello, John."

They smiled at each other, then the odd moment of friendliness caused them to break eye contact.

"Chai latte! With Soy! For Porsha!" The barista yelled out from behind the espresso machine.

Porsha grabbed her drink. "Thanks again, John."

She walked over to her usual seat in the corner, pulling out a chair, and opening her book. Moments later, she felt the presence of someone walking toward her table. She looked up, and it was John.

"Hey, all the tables are taken. Do you mind if I sit here?" He asked, holding his iced coffee in his hand.

"Umm... Sure. Go ahead."

He sat his backpack down on the floor and proceeded to take a seat next to her. He pulled out his laptop and textbook. Porsha realized he was a student, which she figured. This coffee shop was a hot spot for students who went to Georgetown University. The book he pulled out was on Psychology.

"You go to GU?" She asked.

"Yeah. You?"

"No. I went to UDC for a bit but took some time off." She looked at his book again. "You're studying to be a psychologist?"

"Child psychologist, yes."

Porsha loved kids, she wanted to be a teacher. She took a break from getting her bachelor's degree when her mother got sick. She was a few credits away from graduating when her mother passed away a year ago and hadn't been back since. She planned on going back this fall.

"You studied psychology too?" He asked.

"No, I'm planning on being a teacher. Middle school kids preferably."

"That's awesome. The mind of a child is important. They are our future, after all." John said.

"You're absolutely right!" Said Porsha. They shared a moment of smiles, and Porsha couldn't help but notice that John was quite attractive. She had never really been into white guys, but he seemed different. A little annoying, but sweet, and clearly smart. She went back to reading her book. While reading, John admired her looks. Her tight coils pulled back into a ponytail, her edges curling at the sides. Her brown skin, glowing. His admiration of her beauty was suddenly interrupted by her phone ringing. Porsha saw that it was Brittney and answered.

"Hey, Britt!... Yeah, I'm still meeting up with you later. Oh, I wanna talk to you about the center, I have a plan!... Okay, bye!" She hung up and continued to read her book.

They sat there, quiet. Porsha immersed in her reading, and John, busy studying. But every now and then, they would check each other out. Porsha stealing glances and John smelling her coconut oil conditioner. Two hours later, Porsha packed up to get ready to meet up with Brittney.

"Well, it was nice to meet you, again, John. Bye." She got up from her seat and headed toward the door. John got up, leaving his belongings at the table, to catch her before she left.

"Hey Porsha, wait a sec!" He called out to her as she opened the door. She turned around, caught off guard. He walked up to her. "I know I don't really know you that well, but I was wondering if you'd like to come to a party tomorrow night?"

Porsha was shocked. She was trying to figure out if this guy she had basically just met was asking her on a date.

"A party?" She asked.

"Yeah. It's nothing extreme. I mean, I know it's kind of weird for me to ask but…"

"Yes. Sure."

John's facial expression grew excited. He wasn't exactly expecting her to say yes. "Really?"

"Yeah. What's your number?" Porsha pulled out her phone. He gave her his number, and she put him in her contacts. "See you tomorrow night. Bye John." She quickly ran toward the station to catch the train back to the southside. John stood there, waving, watching her leave, before going back inside, smiling from ear to ear.

***

Back on the southside of the city, Porsha sat on the stoop at Brittney's house, as she braided her friend's hair. "So, about my plan to save the rec center, I think we should protest." She told Brittney.

"Sounds like a good idea to me."

"Maybe we'll draw the attention of local news stations. We can tell everyone how much the Riley Gibbs center means to the community. Maybe we can get support from people outside the community."

"Yeah, you know those liberal white folks love a good brown people protest." Brittany laughed.

"Girl you're a trip! But you're right though." Porsha almost forgot to tell Brittney about John. "Speaking of white liberals, I met a guy."

Brittney paused in the middle of a braid. "A guy?" She was intrigued.

"Yeah, his name is john. He goes to GU. I met him at the coffee shop yesterday. He invited me to a party."

"Is he cute?" Brittney asked, interrupting Porsha's braiding while she waited for an answer.

"Yeah, he is." Porsha smiled at the thought of his blue eyes.

"Oooh! look at you! Is he rich?"

"Oh my God, I don't know!" Porsha nudged Brittney playfully.

"Well, I wanna tag along to this party. Just to check him out. You don't know these people."

"Brit, I'll be fine! I don't need you babysitting me all night. Besides, he invited me. It would be impolite to bring someone else."

Brittany rolled her eyes. "Babysitting? Hmm, sounds like you really like this guy. He must be rich."

Porsha laughed. "Shut up!" She nudged Brittany in the leg. "Look, I promise I'll give you all the details after."

"I guess so, just text me if you need me. You know I'll pop up quick!"

"Alright." Porsha agreed, still giggling at her best friend's saucy humor. "So, back to the protest. Spread the word around. Just make sure my dad doesn't hear about it. You know him, I don't want him getting involved." Porsha's dad being a cop, wouldn't approve of her plans, but she was doing it with or without his approval.

***

Porsha quickly searched her closet for her gold wedged heels. The party John had invited her to, started an hour ago. She was wearing her tight yellow romper with the deep V-neck, that complimented her shoulders and breasts. "Where are those damn shoes?" She was getting annoyed by all her closet clutter, tossing things left and right. She heard a buzzing sound coming from her cell phone, and she figured it was probably Brittany. She walked over to her bed to grab her cell phone to check the message. It was John.

John: *Hey, hope I see you tonight.*

Porsha was surprised. The only other time he texted her was to give her the address for the party. She wasn't expecting this. It was random but sweet.

Porsha: *Hey. Yeah, I'll be there.* :)

She felt like the smile emoji was being a little too flirty.

John: :)

Was he flirting now? Porsha smiled at her phone.

Porsha: :) :)

John: *Lol… are we flirting now?*

Now Porsha felt like she got a little too carried away with the smiling emojis. "Probably shouldn't have sent that double smiley." Although she was having a bit of fun, she decided to end their little back and forth play since they were meeting up at the party in a little while.

Porsha: *I'll see you in a bit, ok.*
John: *K.*

She tossed her phone back on her bed and went back to searching for her shoes. After about two more minutes of looking she finally found them. She put them on and went into her bathroom to fix her hair before she left for the party.

***

2939 K street NW is what the text read. This was the spot. The house was nice, one of the nicest homes she had seen in this part of the city. She walked up to the front door and knocked. At that moment, she became nervous, realizing that she would stick out like a sore thumb at this party. In the years that she's gone to that coffee shop on GU campus, she could recall seeing maybe five black people. One being a janitor. She felt that calling or texting John to meet her outside probably would've been a good idea, but it was too late. Someone had already come to the door. It was a brunette white girl with a bob haircut. She had a drink in her hand and a small poodle under her arm. She looked at Porsha with glaring eyes. She was drunk and immediately walked away soon after opening the door, without even saying a word.

Porsha stepped in, looking around. The room was full of young college students, all white and looked as if they came from money. Which was obvious anyway. Most GU students came from comfortably middle-class homes or better. She stood not too far from the door, trying to scope out the place and spot John. She pulled out her phone and began to text him, when someone approached her from the right, placing his hand on her shoulder.

"You came! I was beginning to think you stood me up." It was John. He grinned, handing her a drink. "I wasn't sure what you liked, so I just got you some vodka."

"Vodka's fine." She smiled back at him, taking the glass. They sipped their drinks, standing awkwardly for a minute not knowing what else to say to break the ice.

"You look amazing. Nice outfit."

"Thanks. You look nice too." She tugged at his nice plaid collar.

"Oh, let me introduce you to some of my friends." He guided her toward another room where more people were drinking and socializing. They approached a tall, tanned white guy with dark brunette hair, who was laughing and talking with a few others. Porsha checked him out. He was wearing a sweater vest. Porsha was no fashionista, but a sweater vest? She gagged silently on the inside. That screamed bad news.

"John! Hey, who's your friend?" He greeted, intrigued by his friend's guest, with one hand in his pocket, and sipping his drink with the other.

"This is Porsha."

"Well hello, Porsha, nice to meet you. I'm Thomas. Just call me Tom." He smiled and extended his hand to her. She shook his hand. He seemed like a genuinely nice guy, just like John.

"Nice to meet you." She replied in a soft voice.

"So, how did you two meet one another? I've never seen her around campus. Surely she's not a GU student." He said to John while sipping his drink.

"Umm, no she isn't. I met her at the coffee shop near the library." John looked at Porsha, smiling.

"Ah, I see. Does she go to school nearby?"

Porsha was becoming a little bothered by his questions, and the fact that he was addressing John, not her. "I attend UDC. But I'm a regular at the coffee shop."

Tom's facial expression became uninterested. "UDC? Figures. I assume you're from the southside of town?"

Porsha went from being slightly bothered to full-on offended. "Actually, yes I am." She replied with a hint of attitude.

"I've been to the southside once. My dad's in the process of buying a property over there. Some run-down rec center. We're turning it into condos." Tom told her. Porsha's eyes grew wide as she experienced a rush of anger. Here she was, standing in front of the person who was responsible for the demise of a place she loved. "That place is a dump. That whole neighborhood used to be a dump. But don't worry, in a few years you'll hardly recognize it." Tom continued.

"That dump is my home! That rec center has been a staple of our community for years!" Porsha yelled.

John was becoming uncomfortable with the tension between Porsha and Tom. "Umm, Hey, maybe we should go grab another drink?" John asked her, with his hand on her back, trying to guide her away from the conversation.

"Well, your home was in desperate need of change. People like me are making that happen. You should thank us." Said Tom.

"Thank You? For pricing my people out of our own neighborhoods? Asshole!" Porsha threw her drink on Tom and stormed off.

"Not cool man," John said to Tom right before running after Porsha. She was already outside when he caught up to her. "Porsha, wait!"

She stopped walking and turned around. "What?" She asked angrily.

"I'm sorry about Tom. He's kind of an asshole."

"Kind of?!"

"Ok... he's a huge asshole. I'm sorry." John scratched his head, feeling guilty. He was embarrassed by his friend's treatment of Porsha. He walked closer toward her. "Really, I am sorry."

Porsha wasn't mad at him but felt that if those were the type of people John associated with, then she and him couldn't possibly be friends.

"It's not your fault." She let out a huge sigh. "Look, John, I think you're really cute. You're sweet and everything, but I just think we're two completely different people."

"So, we can't be friends because my friends are assholes?"

"It's not just that... you wouldn't understand."

"I'd like to."

This caught Porsha by surprise. She wasn't expecting him to push this hard. She could tell he liked her and figured giving him a second chance wouldn't hurt. After all, he did come after her. If he was an asshole he would've just let her leave. "Let me show you something."

"Alright... where?" He asked, curious but ready to go wherever she was headed.

"My side of town. But, I think we should get an Uber. It's a little late for the train."

***

Back on the southside of town, they were dropped off in front of the Riley Gibbs Rec Center. They got out of the car, and Porsha walked him toward the front door.

"So, this is the place? The one Tom's dad is buying?" John asked, looking up at the building as they sat down on the steps.

"Yes. This center has been here since the '60s. There's not a soul under fifty in the neighborhood who didn't love this place as a kid. It was like peace in the middle of chaos. It's the one place the gangs wouldn't come near. They knew better. Not only that, but public figures have even given speeches here. This place has way more significance than a place to play." Porsha began to get emotional. "Now, it's all going to be gone in three weeks."

John was speechless. He didn't know how to respond. "I'm sorry. I know it sucks to see a place you care about torn down."

"Do you really? I bet all the nice houses in your suburban hometown are bought by corporations all the time, while people you know and care about are displaced." Porsha said sarcastically.

John gave her a questionable look. "What do think? I'm some rich kid from a loaded family who went to prep school and ate caviar for breakfast?" Porsha looked at him. "Well, I'm not." He continued. "When my dad died, my mom worked two jobs to put me through private school. Thanks to that school, I was able to get an academic scholarship to attend GU."

Porsha was shocked. She felt guilty for having her own preconceived assumptions about him. "Your mom sounds like a hard-working woman." She said softly. They shared a moment of silence.

"Me and my friends are having a protest to save the center. It's going to be the day after tomorrow. "Porsha told him. "I don't even know why I'm telling you this…"

"I'm there!" John said abruptly.

"What? The protest?"

"Yeah, I wanna join. I wanna help." He sounded very enthusiastic.

Porsha felt that there was no harm in letting him join. "Alright. Are you sure? Seems like it would be a conflict of interest, with your friend being involved."

"I don't care about what he thinks. I can think for myself."

"Good." She said, pleased with his response. They smiled at each other. John couldn't help but admire her. She had her hair in that high bun with the loose curls hanging in the back and on the sides, and that coconut conditioner smelled amazing. He loved looking at her. He wasn't sure where things were headed between them, but it felt like the perfect opportunity to do what he had wanted to do since the moment he shared a table with her at the coffee shop. He leaned in for a kiss. She wasn't expecting it but embraced it, which let John know the feeling was mutual.

***

It was the day of the protest. Porsha grabbed her sneakers from the closet, quickly put them on, and headed out the door. Her father had already left, so the coast was clear. Brittany spread the word and got nearly every youth from the southside to participate. When she arrived at city hall, where the protest was being held, the crowd was huge. The turnout was amazing. She caught up with Brittany, who was dressed in all black and ready to go with her megaphone in hand.

"Why are you dressed like you're ready for war?" Porsha asked.

"Well, you never know. Right?" Brittany replied humorously.

"Oh, look! There he is!" Porsha yelled. It was John. She noticed him standing in the crowd. She held her hand up, calling for his attention. "John! Over here!"

"That's him? That's the guy?" Brittany watched as he walked closer toward them. "Oh, he is a cutie. But why is he here? This isn't a date."

"He wanted to come. I said it was okay." Porsha told her.

"Hey!" John got close and went in for a hug. Porsha welcomed him with open arms.

"Britt, this is John. John, this is my best friend Brittany." Porsha introduced them.

"Hi, nice to meet you," John said to Brittany, extending his hand.

"Same." She shook his hand.

"I'm glad you came. It's nice to see you." Porsha expressed.

"Couldn't miss it. Or you." John blushed a little as Porsha smirked, her face wearing a huge grin.

Brittany quickly came in between their sweet little moment. "That's enough you too. We've got work to do." She pulled up her megaphone and began shouting "MAYOR JACKSON! SAVE OUR CENTER! WE KNOW YOU'RE THERE! WE KNOW YOU HEAR US!" Porsha and John, along with the rest of the crowd followed with a chant.

An hour had gone by, and the protest had attracted the local news stations, which is exactly what Porsha wanted. Everything seemed to be going smoothly until a black SUV with police vehicles arrived.

"What the hell?" Porsha was pissed.

"Oh, they better not start! This a peaceful protest! We have a right to be here!" Brittany snapped.

"It's probably my dad. Porsha said. She knew he'd find out eventually, especially with the news stations covering it. She tried to get a good look at the SUV. "With who? I'm not sure."

John looked closer at the vehicle approaching, getting a strange feeling about the visitors. "I think I know."

The cars pulled to the side of the street, which was blocked by the protesters. Porsha's father Brian got out of one of the police vehicles. The doors of the SUV opened and out walked an older white male, who looked to be about fifty. Behind him, another gentleman got out. It was Tom.

"Oh great! This asshole!" Porsha shouted. Her father spotted her, and began to approach her, she could tell he was mad.

"What are you doing here? Don't tell me this was all your idea!" He shouted at his daughter.

"Yes, it was! I'm an adult! I can do whatever I want!"

"These things don't do anything but start trouble! Let's go before anything escalates. We're shutting this down now!" Other protesters heard him and started getting angry. The shouting got louder, they weren't giving up. John approached Tom, who was standing by the vehicle, with a smug look on his face.

"Well look who it is, Johnny boy. You're hanging out in the slums now?" He laughed.

"Why are you here Tom? These people aren't breaking any laws. They have every right to be here."

"Well, these people are getting in the way of business. Why do you care so much anyway? Don't tell me, it's that girl isn't it?"

"So, what if it is?"

"You get a little taste of brown sugar and suddenly you're a bleeding heart now? Classic!" Tom thought all of this was hilarious. "I always knew you were a joke."

John was livid. "I always knew you were a racist piece of garbage. You're a daddy's boy, and you're scum."

Tom punched him square in the face. John clenched his nose, tumbling to the ground. Porsha saw what had happened and ran over to him. "John! Are you alright!" She kneeled to comfort him, clenching his nose with her fingers to stop the bleeding. "What the hell is wrong with you!" She shouted at Tom.

The camera crew from one of the news stations caught the assault on camera. Once it got out, that the son of a wealthy businessman had assaulted a protester, it wouldn't look good for Tom's father. The protesters began to get rowdy, yelling obscenities at Tom and his father. They became intimidated and didn't want to deal with the pressure from reporters, so they got back in the SUV and left the scene. Brian dispatched an ambulance for John, whose nose was gushing blood from the hit.

Another hour had passed, and the crowd started to thin out. "Well, we did what we could. I think we should go home now." Porsha suggested. After getting taken care of in the ambulance, John decided to press charges against Tom.

"Don't worry, everything will work out. Organize another protest if you have to. I have faith in you. Besides, your protest is trending on social media. Everyone in school knows about what Tom did. The mayor may even issue a statement. Something tells me your rec center might be okay."

Porsha lit up with happiness. She placed her arms around John and hugged him tightly. "Thanks for being supportive. I appreciate you being here today."

"Of course." He hugged her back. "You know what I would love right now?"

"Yeah?" Porsha asked.

"Iced coffee."

She laughed. "That sounds good. But maybe we can go to a different coffee shop this time?"

"Sounds good to me."

Andrea: A Sleeping Beauty Retelling

"Be careful, if you pop one of those things, it'll wake the baby," Michelle told her husband Charles as he blew up pink balloons, preparing for their baby shower. They had planned to have it a few days earlier, but Michelle had gone into labor earlier than they had expected. She gave birth to a beautiful baby girl, named Andrea. They decided to go forward with the celebration when she got home from the hospital, allowing friends and family to see baby Andrea.

"Don't worry, I got this, you just relax," Charles told her, as he blew up more balloons.

"Don't you have work to do? Your election is in two weeks. Why not let the maids take care of the decorations?"

"Work can wait. Besides, I want to do this. Let the maids take care of the house before the guests arrive."

Charles's phone started to ring. He grabbed it to see who it was, and his face became concerned.

"Who is it? You don't look very happy." Asked his wife.

"It's her." His voice reeked of fear. "I already told her she isn't welcome, but she won't stop calling me."

Michelle began to get worried. "You think she'll show up? What if she does?"

"She won't. She knows I'll have my guards throw her out of here and she'll be spending the night in a cell."

Juanita Bonèt was the eldest sister of Mayor Charles Bonèt, and far from a family favorite. Ten years earlier, Juanita was suspected of putting a death juju on their father, to inherit the family fortune. After the death of their father, a will was discovered. He was leaving the family fortune to Charles and leaving nothing to Juanita. This angered her, and she hatched a plan to kill Charles. He found out, but before he could confront her, she disappeared. When the news spread of his wife's pregnancy, he started getting calls and messages from Juanita, who wanted to come to the baby shower. Charles refused and threatened her if she were to ever come around again. But this didn't stop her from calling constantly.

Charles turned his phone off and went to go grab a drink. The thought of his sister coming back made him uneasy. He decided to increase security just in case.

***

At 3 pm, their home was filled with guests from all over Louisiana to celebrate the birth of baby Andrea. The dining room was filled with gifts, everyone was happy and enjoying themselves, admiring Bonèt 's new bundle of joy. Suddenly, Charles felt an odd presence, like something was wrong. The house began to shake, and everyone started to panic. Michelle grabbed Andrea and held her tightly. The odd presence Charles felt began to get closer. He turned around and couldn't believe what he was seeing. His sister.

"Security!" He yelled. But no one came.

"Oh, brother. It's so good to see you. It's been so long." Juanita glared at him with an evil smile stretched across her dark face. She was dressed in rags from head to toe and looked as if she hadn't bathed in weeks.

"SECURITY! WHERE IS SECURITY?" Charles demanded.

"Oh, they are taking a nap. They won't be bothering us. Don't worry." Said Juanita, still smiling sadistically. She looked over at Michelle, who was holding baby Andrea. "My beautiful niece! Give her to me!" She demanded.

"NO!" Michelle yelled.

"DON'T YOU GO NEAR HER!" Screamed Charles.

Juanita turned around, facing her brother. "Unless you want me to kill you, and everyone else in this room, including your child, I suppose you better let me see her."

Charles knew that Juanita had always been involved in powerful black magic and could make things happen if she wanted to. Bad things. He didn't have a choice. "You can hold her, for a minute."

Juanita clapped in excitement and reached over to grab the baby from Michelle. Juanita held the baby in her arms, while The Bonèt 's and all the guests watched in terror. "Look at you, just as beautiful as your auntie." She said to Andrea. "Unfortunately, I can't stay, but I won't leave without giving you my gift."

Charles and Michelle looked confused.

"Juanita reached into her pocket and pulled out red sand. She sprinkled it over Andrea's mouth. She whispered something in the baby's ear, kissed her on the cheek, and handed her back to Michelle.

"What did you just do to my daughter?" Charles asked, frightened.

"I gave her a gift. On her sixteenth birthday, she will fall into a deep sleep. She will sleep for eternity. Only in her dreams will she exist."

"NO!" Charles yelled with fury. Michelle started crying, and all the guests stood in awe.

Juanita snapped her fingers, and all the guests in the room except Charles and Michelle fell asleep. "None of them will remember a thing." She laughed.

"YOU EVIL BITCH!" I'LL KILL YOU!" Charles charged at her but with a flick of the hand, she sent him flying across the room.

"Goodbye, brother. It was a pleasure seeing you again." The house began to shake, and within seconds, Juanita was gone.

All the guests began to wake up, confused and disoriented. Michelle and Charles just stood there in disbelief, not knowing what to say, or think.

***

Sixteen years later

Andrea rushed downstairs to see her birthday gift. Her parents had been keeping it a secret for weeks, but she knew they had gotten her the car that she wanted. Her parents were still sleeping, but she rushed outside barefoot and anxious. As soon as she saw the silver Lexus sitting in the driveway with a big pink bow, she screamed with joy.

"Looks like she's up." Said Michelle, who was awakened by the screams. She leaned over and kissed her husband. "Good morning." He didn't respond, but he was awake. "Honey, I know you're worried, I am too. But it's her birthday." She said to him.

"I know." He said, still facing the wall. It was the day the curse would take his daughter's life. Not literally, but figuratively. It was the day Charles and Michelle dreaded for sixteen years. They listened as Andrea yelled from the driveway, thanking them for her gift.

"Let's go wish our daughter a happy birthday. I'll put breakfast on." Michelle got out of bed and headed downstairs. Charles didn't budge. He knew that today would be the last day he would see his daughter smiling, laughing, happy. Living her life.

When he finally went downstairs to join his family for breakfast, his daughter immediately got up from her seat to throw her arms around him, hugging him tightly. "Thank you so much, dad! I love you! The car is amazing!"

"You're welcome, baby girl. Happy birthday."

His daughter noticed that he didn't sound so happy. "What's wrong?" Andrea asked, concerned. Charles and his wife looked at each other. "I'm fine sweetie." He told Andrea.

"Alright, just asking." Andrea smiled at her father.

Her parents never told her about her aunt Juanita, or the curse. They wanted their daughter to live her best life. They never enrolled her in school, she had a private tutor since the age of five. Andrea was a loner who never really made any friends. Except one. A girl named Piper, who was also homeschooled. They had been friends since the age of six, and inseparable ever since.

"I can't wait to show Piper my new car!" Said Andrea while she texted her friend. "We're going to the mall today."

"The mall? But your mother and I are taking you to dinner." The last thing her father wanted was his daughter out of his sight on this day.

"We won't be there all day. Just for a while. We can still do dinner later. Please, dad?" She begged.

"I just really wanted all of us to spend the day together."

"Let her go. Two hours. Then we can have the rest of the day." Said Michelle. "It's alright Charles, she'll be fine."

"Umm… jeez guys I'm just going to the mall, I'm not dying," Andrea said jokingly.

Her parents looked at each other with disappointment on their faces. They felt guilty for keeping the curse a secret. But they didn't know how they could ever tell her.

"Sure. Have fun. We'll see you in two hours." Charles agreed.

Andrea ran up to her room to call Piper and tell her about her new car. Her parents didn't know how to feel. It was 9 am and the curse hadn't taken effect yet. Maybe it wouldn't? Maybe, Andrea would be safe after all.

***

"The car is really nice, Andrea." Said Piper as she sat on the passenger's side while Andrea drove to the mall.

"I know right!" Andrea's curly brown hair blew in the wind while she had all the windows down. Her silver Saturn ring sunglasses went perfectly with her magenta lipstick. "My parents are amazing!"

They parked near the entrance and went inside. Their first stop was a frozen yogurt place that was Andrea's favorite. She ordered a chocolate brownie swirl and Piper ordered strawberry. They took a seat at a nearby table. Piper stared at Andrea as she took large bites of her treat.

"Andrea, I wanted to talk to you about something." Piper began to get nervous, fiddling with her spoon.

"Oh good, I wanted to talk to you about something as well. But you can go first."

"Well, we've been friends for a long time. We've only ever been around each other."

"Yeah..." Andrea gulped down her frozen treat, waiting to hear what Piper had to say.

Piper was struggling to put her thoughts into words. She had a secret that she had been wanting to tell Andrea for a while now. "I care about you, a lot. I got you a gift for your birthday, and I was just waiting for the right time to give it to you." Piper paused. "Andrea… I-"

Suddenly, there was a loud thump. Andrea's frozen yogurt spilled all over the floor. Next to her unconscious body.

"Andrea!" Piper yelled out, jumping out of her chair, and rushing to help her friend. She was unconscious. "Andrea! Wake up! What's going on!" She shook her frantically. "Someone, call 911!" The cashier panicked and ran to call for help. Piper sat there holding up Andrea's head, crying, confused and worried to death. Within ten minutes an ambulance had arrived. Andrea was rushed to the nearest hospital, with Piper by her side.

When they arrived at the hospital, Piper sat by Andrea's bedside, waiting for her parents to arrive. When they got there, Piper was distraught. She tried to explain that she had no idea what happened. That Andrea just passed out. Charles and Michelle just stood there, looking at their daughter. They were at a loss for words.

"We knew this day would come. It's my fault, I should've protected her that day." Charles said in a faint voice. Piper didn't understand.

"What are you talking about Mr. Bonèt?"

He stared at his daughter with tears in his eyes as he held her limp hand. "Sixteen years ago, my sister put a curse on Andrea. On her sixteenth birthday, my baby girl would fall into a deep sleep, forever. She will never wake up." Piper couldn't believe what she was hearing.

"Black magic?" She whispered with her hand over her mouth. In Louisiana, hearing about these practices was common for most folks who grew up near the bayou. But most people only knew little jujus and hexes. Nothing as strong as what Andrea was under. Piper knew this was the work of a powerful woman, and there was nothing they could do. "No! It can't be! Not her! She doesn't deserve this!" Piper cried.

"I know. I wish I could change things. I wish it could've been me instead." Charles sat there, in more pain than any father could imagine.

***

Months passed by, as they watched her sleep day in and day out. Charles and Michelle brought Andrea home a few days after she had gone to the hospital. The doctors couldn't find anything medically wrong with Andrea, and her parents wouldn't tell them about the curse. So, they took her home. In her room, she slept, peacefully. Piper came to visit her every day. She was the only one besides Charles and Michelle who were allowed near Andrea. Charles spent days and nights searching for his sister, in hopes that she would take back the curse. But he didn't find anything. No signs of her at all.

Two years passed by, and Andrea hadn't aged a day. Still, her parents and her best friend were by her side. One night, while Charles was sleeping in a chair next to his daughter's bed, the house began to shake. Charles was startled out of his sleep by the sound of a flower vase falling to the floor and breaking. Michelle came running in to see what was going on, along with Piper who had spent the night. Suddenly, there she was. Juanita.

"Did you miss me, dear brother?" She said, with that evil smirk on her face. She looked different this time. Older, and frail, like she was sick.

"Juanita… It's really you." Charles uttered. Juanita walked over to Andrea's bed, and leaned over, moving a stray curly hair from Andrea's face. "You stay away from her!" Michelle demanded.

"Hush woman! You should be happy to see me."

"Juanita, please. Take back the curse. Spare our daughter. You can curse me instead." Charles begged.

"Now what fun would that be?" Juanita laughed. "Don't worry. Today is your lucky day. I've come to take back the curse." She ran her hand across Andrea's soft brown cheek. "Under one condition."

Charles and Michelle didn't like the sound of this. "What condition?" Asked Charles.

"I want her youth, in exchange for my dying, aging body."

"NO! OVER MY DEAD BODY!" Shouted Michelle.

"That can be arranged." Juanita snapped back.

"Please, stop. Juanita, I beg you. Just take back the curse or let her be." Said Charles.

"I didn't have to come here. I'm doing you a favor. If I want, I can kill the both of you, take her youth, and let her lie here until she dies. Your choice."

"NO!" Shouted Piper, crying for her best friend's life.

"Have it your way then." Juanita stepped back, opening both arms, and mumbling in another language. The house began to shake again. Piper looked over at the broken glass on the floor and picked up the largest piece. She charged at Juanita and shoved the large piece of glass into her chest. Right in her heart. The house stopped shaking, and Juanita screamed out in pain. She fell to the floor, her lifeless body, sitting in a small pool of her blood. Charles and Michelle stood there, in shock. Piper dropped the glass, in disbelief of what she had just done, tears rolling down her eyes. She looked at Andrea, who was still lying there. She walked over toward her and whispered in her ear.

"I love you." Piper then placed a gentle kiss on Andrea's lips. Charles and Michelle gathered around their daughter. Juanita was dead, and the curse was still there. They all felt hopeless. That was until Charles felt Andrea's hand move. He couldn't believe it. "Andrea?" He said in a soft, hopeful voice. Suddenly, her eyes opened.

"Andrea! I can't believe it!" Charles jumped in excitement as they all cheered happily.

Andrea sat up. "Mom, dad, Piper. What happened to me?" She looked over at the dead body on the floor. "Oh my God! Who is that?"

They all looked at each other. "There is a lot we need to tell you. But right now, we're just happy to see your beautiful face." Her father hugged her tightly. So, did her mother.

***

Later that night, Charles and Michelle explained everything to Andrea and got rid of Juanita's body. Andrea took it all well and understood why her parents kept it all a secret. She was just happy it was all over. They all were.

Andrea and Piper sat on the porch, sitting in silence. Piper reached into her pocket, and pulled out a small necklace, with the letter *P* hanging from the end. "I never got a chance to give you your birthday gift." She said to Andrea. She then pulled out a necklace she was already wearing, identical to the one she was giving to Andrea, except hers had the letter *A* hanging from it. "I got this necklace a few months before I got yours. I wanted it to be a surprise. I love you, Andrea, I always have. I just never knew how to tell you, or what you would say."

Andrea smiled, and reached for her gift, she stood up and turned around, lifting her hair as Piper placed the necklace around Andrea's neck. She twirled the end of the necklace with her thumb. "I love it Piper, and I love *you,* too."

Even the strongest black magic in the world was no match for true love.

Briana: A Beauty and the Beast Retelling

"Don't forget to pick up flour on your way home from school!" Briana's mother yelled from the top of the stoop.

"Yeah, I know. Bye, ma!" Briana replied, annoyed by her mother's constant reminder to pick up flour. This was the third time she had mentioned it since Briana woke up that morning. With her tote bag full of textbooks, Briana took her time walking to school. She loved listening to the loud cars pass by, and the smell of flowers blossoming as Spring made its way through the city.

"Morning Briana!" Greeted Mr. Bernard from the corner barbershop as he swept hair away from his front door.

"Good morning Mr. Bernard! Working hard today?" Briana greeted cheerfully with a huge smile.

"Hardly. Same ol' same ol' with me." He replied. "You have a good day at school now ya hear?"

"I'll try." She waved and continued walking to school. He waved back and continued his sweeping. As Briana approached the next street, she noticed a group of guys hanging out in front of a convenience store. Her anxiety kicked in, and she was worried that one of them would say something to her as she passed by. She had her head down and started walking faster as she passed them. One of the guys, wearing a white tank top had his eye on her.

"Hey girl!" He called out to her. Briana knew this would happen. She clenched her bag tighter and continued walking. "Hey, girl! I know you heard me!" He shouted again.

Briana stopped and turned around. The boy was walking toward her. The last thing she wanted to deal with was harassment from one of the hood boys.

"Come on man, leave that girl alone." One of the boy's friends said. It was a tall young man, with long dreadlocks that reached his waist. He was very dark, with a huge scar on the right side of his face. While the other guys seemed amused by their friend's harassment of Briana, the one with the dreadlocks didn't seem amused at all.

"What? You think you're too good to talk to me or something?" The guy asked her aggressively. She didn't respond.

"Man, I told you to leave that girl alone!" The dreadlock gentleman stood there with his arms crossed. His friend looked back at him, then looked at Briana. "Man forget you." He brushed her off and walked back toward his friends. Briana didn't waste any time hurrying off to get to school. She arrived a little tired out from powerwalking the rest of the way there. She was paranoid that the group of guys might have followed her, but thankfully they didn't. She walked inside the building with only a few minutes left before the bell rang for first period. She rushed to her locker to put her books away and grabbed the ones she needed.

"Briana, what's going on?" Before she could close her locker, Gerard was standing over her, his arm leaning on the locker next to hers. He had a vain, smug look on his face, a look he always wore whenever he approached her. "What are you up to after school today?" He asked, grabbing a book from her locker.

"Nothing." She replied, uninterested. Gerard had a crush on her since sophomore year. He had attempted to ask her out before, and she declined every time. But he never gave up. He approached her at least twice a week, and she brushed him off every single time.

"Is that all you do? Read?" He asked, flipping through the book he grabbed.

"No." She said, annoyed. She grabbed the book from him and tossed it back into her locker. "I'm going to be late for class." She slammed it closed and tried to brush past him, but he blocked her way.

"Come on, why won't you go out with me? I'm fly, I've got money. Girls try to get at me every day but here I am, trying to get at you. So, what's up?" He stood there, towering over her with his broad shoulders. His light brown skin smelled like expensive cologne, and his fade was fresh like he had a barber on hand every morning. Gerard wasn't an unattractive boy, but Briana wasn't a fan of his personality. He was self-centered, obnoxious, and treated anyone who wasn't at his level of popularity like garbage. The only reason he wasn't a complete ass to Briana, was because he wanted to date her.

"I'm going to be late for class." She said again before slightly pushing him aside and walking away. The one thing she detested about school was having to deal with his never-ending advances.

***

Briana made her way to the 9th street market when school let out. It was only two blocks away from her school, and her mother only bought groceries from that market when she couldn't make it to the regular grocery store. Briana approached the store and immediately felt a huge lump in her throat. The guys she had trouble with that morning were standing there, posted up outside the store.

"Oh no, ugh," Briana mumbled. The library was across the street, so she figured she could go there and read for a while and maybe they would be gone when she came back.

She made a B-line for the library before one of the guys could notice her. It was empty, besides the homeless men who used it as shelter during the day, and a few senior citizens listening to audiobooks. She walked to the Adult Romance section, which was straight to the back. She browsed the first few rows to see if anything new had come in. She picked up a book titled "For the Love of Honey", took a seat, and cracked it open.

About ten minutes in, Briana was startled by two loud bangs coming from outside. It sounded like gunshots, she was pretty sure it was gunshots. She froze, not knowing what to do. She then heard someone running. She looked ahead and that's when she saw him. It was the boy with the scar and dreadlocks. As he ran in her direction, they made eye contact. Briana, not sure how to react just sat there as he sprinted right past her and disappeared behind a bookshelf. Everything had happened so fast and she was puzzled by what she had just seen. Minutes later she noticed two uniformed officers walking into the library. She immediately knew why they were there. The uniformed officers looked around and started walking in her direction. This made her nervous.

"Hello young lady, we're looking for a young man who may have been involved in a robbery attempt across the street. He may have run into this building. Tall, dark complexion with long hair. Have you seen him?" One of the officers asked. He sounded intimidating.

"I... I haven't seen anyone." Briana responded timidly.

"Are you sure?" The officer asked as if he wasn't too confident in her answer.

"Yes."

"Thanks, young lady." The two officers went to check another part of the library and Briana took a deep breath, smacking herself in the head with the book she was holding.

I can't believe I just lied to a cop.

She wanted to get out of there as soon as possible. She closed the book, grabbed her school bag, and went back over to the shelf to put the book back.

"Thanks." A male voice whispered from behind the bookcase. Briana jumped. "Sorry, I didn't mean to scare you." He said softly. Briana walked slowly behind the bookcase. There he was, sitting on the floor.

"You're welcome." She said. "Bye." She turned around to leave, but he stopped her.

"Wait, don't go yet." He said abruptly. She stopped walking and turned around. "The cops are still here. They're most likely posted up outside, to see if I'll come out. Could you wait with me?"

She couldn't believe what he was asking. "Wait with you? Are you crazy! I just lied to the cops, for you. Why? I have no idea. But you should be glad I was nice enough to do that!" She scoffed at him and turned around to leave again.

"I tried to stop him." The young man stood up. Briana stopped walking. "I didn't know he was gonna do it. I tried to talk him out of it, but gunshots went off, and it was too late." Briana turned around to look at him.

"Did anyone get hurt?" She asked.

"I don't think so. I hope not."

She looked him in the eyes, and she wasn't sure why, but something inside of her knew he was telling the truth. "Just let me grab my book." She walked back to the other side of the bookcase to grab the book she was reading before the chaos happened. She placed her bag on the floor and took a seat across from where he was standing. He went to slouch down next to her. He leaned in to get a look at what she was reading.

"Just wait until you get to the sequel." He said. Briana looked over at him. "I read that back in tenth grade. Read part two a few weeks after I finished. It's better than that one."

Briana was taken by surprise. "You've read this?" She asked, with one eyebrow raised. The question came off as a challenge of intelligence more than an actual question.

"What? Is a brother reading that hard to believe?"

"No, I just…" Briana realized that her question came off as snobby, and he had picked up on it. "I just hadn't heard of this book before today. That's all." She pulled the book closer to her face and went back to reading. She felt awkward and was beginning to regret sitting there with him.

"What's your name?" He asked.

For a second, she wasn't sure if she wanted to tell him. "Briana."

"Jamal." He smiled at her, but she hadn't taken her eyes off her book at all. He decided to get up and grab a book from the shelf. He picked up a book titled "A Time Traveler's Love." He sat back down next to her and began reading. Briana glanced over at him while he wasn't looking. This was the first time she had gotten a good look at him. His skin was like dark chocolate, smooth like it too. His dreadlocks didn't look like the other guys' hair in the neighborhood who had locs. His were neat and tightly twisted. He had a mane of long, thick, dark hair that made him quite intimidating. The scar on his face didn't do him any justice either. Without it, he might've been a very attractive young man. But even though he wasn't, something about him was still so appealing to her.

"I've read that one." She said to him, looking over at the book.

"You mean you've read this? No way!" He said in a condescending tone of voice. Briana huffed at him, offended. "Doesn't sound so nice the other way around, does it?" He teased.

"Oh, whatever." She tried to play it off as if she knew he was just teasing. "Anyway, It's a good book."

"I'm sure it is." He grinned at her, and she suddenly felt uncomfortable. Briana wasn't used to having what felt like a flirtatious moment. The only other guys who smiled at her were the old men in the neighborhood, and Gerard, who she couldn't stand. This was unfamiliar for her. She closed her book and stood up.

"I'm gonna go check and see if the cops are still lingering around." She grabbed her bag and walked toward the front of the library to look outside. She didn't see either of the cops who came in, just a cop car across the street at the scene of the shooting, but they must've been inside the store. She went back to tell Jamal the coast was clear. "They're gone."

Jamal stood up, closed his book, and placed it back on the shelf. "I guess this is goodbye then?" He walked closer toward her.

"I guess so." Briana slightly shrugged her shoulders. She looked over at the bookcase. "Are you going to check out the book to finish it? It really is good."

"Nah, I don't check out books. I'd rather not get roasted by my boys. But I'll stay if you stay."

Briana's eyes widened. She wasn't sure of what to say. She hardly knew him, but his presence felt warm. She didn't feel like staying, but she didn't want to say no either. "Okay." She agreed.

He walked back over to pick up the book and sat down at the table this time. Briana sat across from him. She remembered what happened this morning while she was walking to school. "Thanks for what you did this morning."

"Oh yeah, about that. It was nothing. My friend can be an ass. I keep telling him to leave these girls alone. He never listens."

"Well, I'm glad he listened to you that time." She thought about what had happened across the street. "Was he the one that tried to rob the store?"

Jamal gave her a look as if he didn't want to talk about it. "Yeah." He replied, sounding hurt by what his friend had done. "I can't believe I ran. I should've stayed, I should've made him leave. I feel like it's my fault." She looked at Jamal and could tell he was overwhelmed with regret.

"It's not your fault. You had to look out for yourself, and that's what you did." Briana reached over and gently touched his hand to comfort him. This made Jamal feel better, he looked into Briana's eyes and she gazed into his.

"Thank you." He said softly. Briana was beginning to feel awkward again and quickly snatched her hand away. She wanted to change the subject but also wanted to know more about him. She got a good look at the scar on his face. She wasn't sure if it was impolite to ask but felt confident that he was nice enough to not mind if she did.

"What happened to your face?" Briana asked cautiously. This caught Jamal off guard. He was quiet for a few seconds before he answered.

"I was thirteen. Walking home from school, and these gang members tried to rob me. I tried to fight them off, but one of them had a knife. He got me right in the face. I had to get fifteen stitches."

Briana was horrified by the details of his trauma. She had her hands covering her mouth, with her eyes wide. She felt horrible. He paused before he could finish. "I was so ugly, I couldn't go back to school, so I dropped out. The guys you saw me hanging with, they've been my only friends since. That's why I stick around. They're the only people besides my parents who don't look at me like I'm a monster."

"I don't think of you like that. You're not a monster to me."

A slight smile formed across Jamal's face. "You're the first girl in four years to ever be this nice to me, Briana."

"Well, you're the only guy I've come across lately under the age of forty who doesn't treat me like a piece of ass."

"I would never treat you like that." He said, admiring her beauty from across the table. Briana blushed, covering her face with her book. She knew that Jamal was someone that she wanted to keep around. He was sweet and loved to read. She didn't come across too many guys like him in her neighborhood.

They stayed at the library for about two hours, talking, laughing, and reading. They realized that they had more in common with each other than they realized. Jamal offered to walk her home, and she kindly accepted. When they arrived at her house, Jamal didn't hesitate to ask her out. "Maybe we can meet up at the library tomorrow? Check out some audiobooks together?"

"I'd like that. Three-thirty?" She recommended.

"Cool. I'll be there. See ya."

"See ya," Briana smirked. Before she could go inside, Jamal stopped her. "Briana, wait." She turned around, and he walked up to her door. She looked up at him, and he looked down on her, he couldn't take his eyes off of her. He leaned down and kissed her softly. She didn't budge and embraced his kiss. After a few seconds of being entranced by his soft lips, she pushed him away.

"I gotta go. See you tomorrow." She turned to go inside and quickly closed the door. Jamal sprinted away, his face full of Joy. All he could think about was her.

***

The next day, Briana didn't waste any time hurrying to the Library to meet Jamal. She walked around the corner and noticed a crowd and some police vehicles outside of the library. The chaos made her uneasy but curious, so she ran over to see what was going on. Pushing through the crowd, she saw Jamal in handcuffs. She also saw Gerard. Standing nearby with a sinister but satisfied look on his face.

"Jamal! What's going on?" She yelled for him while she ran closer.

"What are you doing here Briana? You know this thug?" Asked Gerard.

"He's not a thug!"

"Well, the authorities and several witnesses disagree. He and his thug friends tried to rob the market across the street. MY market! My family owns that place, the whole building!"

"He didn't do anything!" Briana pleaded.

An officer stood between Briana and Gerard. "Miss, I'm gonna need you to step back." He told her.

"No! He's innocent!" She tried to reason with the officer but knew it wouldn't work.

"Briana it's okay, just go home," Jamal told her calmly. She ran over to hug him. Gerard became disgusted.

"So, this is why you won't go out with me? You like these criminals. Can't say I'm surprised. Trash attracts trash."

This made Briana so angry, she spit on Gerard. He became furious, and smacked her across the face, sending her stumbling to the ground. Still handcuffed, Jamal ran straight for Gerard, tackling him to the ground. An officer had to break up the scuffle, placing Jamal and Gerard both inside separate vehicles. The officers hauled Jamal to the station, and Briana hurried home, to change and go to the station in Jamal's defense.

When she arrived at the station, a clerk told her that Jamal was being questioned, and they would provide her with any information once it became available. She took a seat and waited. About twenty minutes later, Jamal was released. He was so happy to see Briana, that he immediately ran to hug her.

"They let you go? How? Why?" She asked

"My friend confessed to everything. Told them I wasn't involved, and they let me go." Briana was so happy, she hugged him again. An officer who was at the scene earlier had asked Briana if she wanted to press charges against Gerard for assaulting her. She didn't hesitate to say yes.

"After all this is done and over, I want to take you on a real date. Books are optional" Jamal laughed.

Briana smiled and grabbed his hand. "I'd love that."

Here's a Special Treat! Check out the first chapter of Fernando! Available now!

After a year in county jail, a new life on the outside awaits! Nineteen-year-old Amari Davis is a rebellious transgender teen from Georgia with a desperate desire for a fresh start—but being packed off to Brazil to work with her father, a military vet now in the Peace Corps, isn't exactly what she has in mind. Amari struggles to adjust to the new culture and fit in with the locals until she meets Gabriel, a handsome and endearing young man who works with her father. The two are drawn to each other, and as their friendship deepens, Amari's newfound romance tests her resolution to live authentically. If she tells Gabriel the truth about herself, will it push him away forever?

From award-winning author Chanel Hardy, 'Fernando' is a modern, unconventional love story set in the 90's that explores what it means to live as your authentic self, giving love a chance when all seems lost, and to be young and resilient in the face of adversity.

Winter, 1997

Knots formed in the center of Amari's abdomen as she sat on the hospital bed. Soon she would be transferred to the operating room. Her mother Elise stood by her side, grasping her daughters' hand. Elise bowed her head, closed her eyes and spoke softly as she prayed over Amari. After nearly three years of puberty blockers and hormone replacement therapy, it was finally Amari's big day. Getting bottom surgery would mark the beginning of her new life as a fully transitioned transgender woman.

"I can't believe this is actually happening." Amari said. She placed her hand over her stomach. "I'm so nervous."

"Don't be," Elise said. "I'm here. Everything will be fine."

Elise smiled and rubbed Amari's shoulder. It had taken a long time for Elise to come to terms with her daughter's transition. At the age of thirteen, Amari came out as trans to her mother. Elise found breast pads and a tote bag full of makeup hidden in Amari's closet, which led to an emotional breakdown that caused a huge rip in their relationship. Fernando 6 With a lack of support, Amari disobeyed her mother and turned to the street life. She committed petty crimes to afford her hormone medication. The first time Amari was caught shoplifting, Elise found hormone pills in her room. At that moment, she realized that what her daughter was going through was no phase. She set her own feelings aside and decided that she would provide the support Amari needed on her journey to transition, even if she didn't understand it.

"Have you heard from dad?" Amari asked.

Amari looked up at her mother with hopeful eyes. Elise didn't respond. She just nodded with pressed lips. Amari let out a faint sigh. While her father was supportive of her coming out as queer, he wasn't too fond of her coming out as trans. He was even more opposed to her having such a life-changing procedure. Amari felt that he would always subconsciously hold on to the son he always wanted. But despite his opposition, she was having the surgery with or without him.

"He loves you." said Elise as she reassured Amari. "You know that."

"I know." replied Amari.

She smiled weakly. Someone knocked on the door. Elise and Amari looked to see who was there.

"Are we ready to go?" asked a male voice.

The doctor peeked his head inside the patient room.

"Yes." Amari answered.

Her stomach settled as the excitement for her new life set in. The doctor walked in and approached them with his clipboard in hand. "Good." said the doctor. "Let's get you prepped for surgery." Amari laid back and still held on to her mother's hand as the doctor prepared to take her into surgery. They locked eyes. Elise placed her palm on her daughter's chin. This was it.

"Damarion Davis." a male voice called out.

Two men approached the room door. One, being a uniformed police officer. A sharp pain pierced Amari's chest. Her skin prickled.

"Excuse me?" Elise interjected. She inched closer towards Amari. "What do you want with my daughter?"

Her brow furrowed as she observed the two men.

"I'm Detective Porter." said the man in regular clothes.

As he reached into his blazer to pull out his badge, he stared down Amari. "Damarion, you are under arrest for theft and credit card fraud."

The uniformed officer reached for his cuffs and proceeded to Amari.

"What is the meaning of this?" Elisa questioned in a fretful tone. She peered down at her daughter. "Amari, what is happening?"

The look of guilt and regret washed over Amari's face as the officer sat her up and placed the cuffs on her wrists. Her eyes glossed with tears as her whole world imploded. She was so close to starting a new life, and just like that, it was all over before it began.

ABOUT THE AUTHOR

YA/NA author and poet born and raised in the Washington D.C. area. In 2017 Chanel decided to take a leap of faith and follow her dreams of publishing her first book, 'My Colorblind Rainbow' which made the 'In The Margins Award Long List' for YA fiction in 2018. She launched Hardy Publications in September of 2017, working as a free lance writer and literary blogger. She's written for publications such as Women and Words, 25 Hottest Indie Authors Artists Advocates 2020, and CulEpi. With certifications in persuasive writing and public speak ing, TEFL(Teaching English as a Foreign Language) while overseas, Chanel uses her platform to raise awareness for different charities and non-profit organizations, volunteering both locally and internationally, and giving back to the community. Read more at https://www.chardypublications.com/